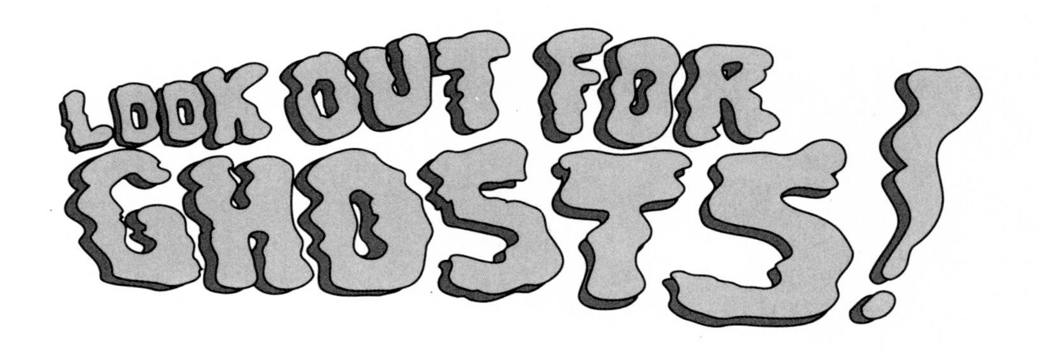
LOOK OUT FOR
GHOSTS!

MAKE THE PICTURES REALLY GLOW!

As you read, hold each page up to a bright light for at least 20 seconds. Then turn off the light and watch the pictures glow!

You can also have fun with this book using a flashlight at night in bed. With the lights out, shine the flashlight directly onto a page for 20 seconds or more. Then switch off the flashlight—and watch the pictures glow in the dark!

A Joshua Morris Book
Published by The Reader's Digest Association, Inc.

Originally published and produced by Arnoldo Mondadori Editore, S.p.A., Milano 1991.

Printed in Italy.
Library of Congress Catalog Card Number: 92-60790
ISBN 0-89577-438-0
10 9 8 7 6 5 4 3 2 1

Annette Tison & Talus Taylor

a Joshua Morris book
from The Reader's Digest Association, Inc.

"Your father and I are going next door for just a little while, so be good."

"We will."

"You can play in the house or in the backyard, but don't go anywhere else. Understand?"

"Yes, Mom."

"Take care of each other now."

"Don't worry."

"Hooray!"

"Now we can do anything we want ...
well, almost."

"What shall we do first?"

"Let's play hide-and-seek in the backyard."

"But ... it's getting dark out there."

"You're not scared, are you?"

"Of course not! I'll hide, and you try to find me."

"Okay. I'll count to ten, starting now. One, two, three, four, five, six, seven, eight, nine, ten! Ready or not, here I come!"

"WOOF! WOOF!"
"Be quiet, Ruff! You'll give us away!"
"WOOF! WOOF! WOOF!"
"Shhhhhhh!"

"Ah, I found you! Why are you looking so worried? What's wrong?"

"N-n-n-nothing's wrong. I just don't want to play hide-and-seek anymore. Let's do something else."

"I know! Let's go into the garage!"

"Well, we're here. What's the matter now?"
"Oh, nothing. I just think we should go inside. We could play in the kitchen."

"Okay, let's make some yuck soup! You get the water, and I'll get the mustard and ketchup and whipped cream and orange juice and pickles. Do you think we need anything else?"

"Yes, we could add ... do you see something strange over by the washing machine?"

"Oh, stop it!"

“Let’s go into the living room.”
“Why?”
“We can pound on the piano.”
“So what are we waiting for?”
“I, er, I can’t find the light switch.
Don’t push!”

“Aaaaaah! Ghosts! There are ghosts everywhere! Heeelp!”
“I don’t see any ghosts! But if it makes you feel better, we can go up to my room.”

"Hurry! I'm telling you, the whole house is haunted! Run, Ruff, run!"

"Will you please slow down? I can't keep up with you!"

"Whew! The door's locked. So there's nothing to be scared about now."

"Look! Over by the window ... it's another ghost, coming to get us!"

"Don't be silly! That's just a streetlamp in the window. Besides, there are no such things as ghosts. I'm tired of all this. Let's get ready for bed."

"That shower looks strange.
Its eyes are watching us.
Can't you see them?"
"No! Now finish brushing your teeth."

"Will you stay with me until I fall asleep? Please?"
"Yes, if you'll stop all this nonsense!"

"And will you leave the light on ... and bring me my teddy bear ... and let Ruff sleep with me ... and kitty ... and my stuffed rabbit ... and—"

"Yes, yes, I'll do anything to keep you quiet! Here's kitty!"

"Hello, children! We're back!"

"Hi, Mom."

"Hi, Mom."

"Is everything all right?"

"Yes, Mom."

"Yes, Mom."

"Good. Sleep tight!"

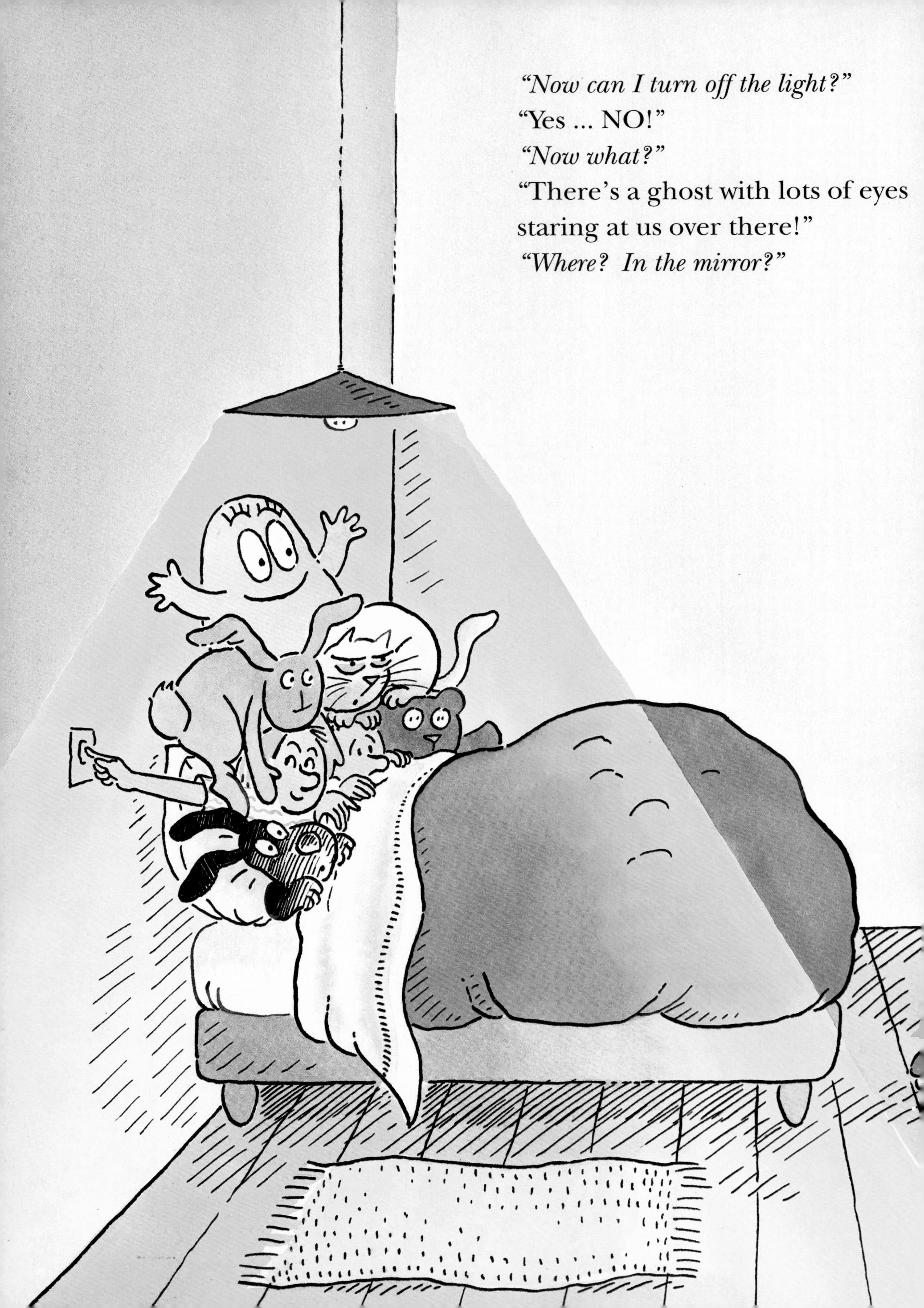

"Now can I turn off the light?"
"Yes ... NO!"
"Now what?"
"There's a ghost with lots of eyes staring at us over there!"
"Where? In the mirror?"

"If that's a ghost, it's a good ghost. It's watching over us. Now go to sleep!"
"All right. Good night."
"Good night."